WINTER RESCUE

To my grandson, Sean—W. D. V.

To Haoyin and Ping—A. Z.

First United States edition 1995

Margaret K. McElderry Books
An imprint of Simon & Schuster Children's Publishing Division
1230 Avenue of the Americas
New York, New York 10020

Text copyright © 1994 by W. D. Valgardson
Illustrations copyright © 1994 by Ange Zhang
First published in Toronto by
Groundwood Books/Douglas & McIntyre Ltd.
The text of this book is set in Janson.
The illustrations were done in colored pencil.

Printed in Hong Kong
1 3 5 7 9 10 8 6 4 2

LIBRARY OF CONGRESS CATALOGING-IN-PUBLICATION DATA
Valgardson, W. D.
[Thor]
Winter rescue / W. D. Valgardson ; illustrated by Ange Zhang.—1st U.S. ed.
p. cm.
Originally published : Thor. Toronto :
Groundwood Books / Douglas & McIntyre © 1994.
Summary: While helping his grandfather, an ice fisherman on frigid
Lake Winnipeg, Thor becomes a hero even braver than his favorite cartoon
superheroes. Includes recipe for a traditional Icelandic-Canadian dessert.
ISBN 0-689-80094-0
[1. Ice fishing—Fiction.   2. Fishing—Fiction.
3. Grandfathers—Fiction.   4. Heroes—Fiction.]
I. Zhang, Ange, ill.   II. Title.
PZ7.V2535Wi   1995   94-48339
[Fic]—dc20   AC

WINTER
RESCUE

W. D. VALGARDSON

illustrated by

ANGE ZHANG

Margaret K. McElderry Books

T H O R had come to visit his grandparents for the Christmas holidays, but all he wanted to do was watch television. He talked to his grandmother and grandfather about the adventures he saw on television. He talked about his favorite heroes and their great deeds.

Thor's grandfather was a fisherman. He spent his days setting and lifting nets out on Lake Winnipeg.

Friday night Grandfather announced, "My hired man, Ben, is sick. I don't know what I'll do. I've got to get my nets set."

"Hire someone else," Grandmother said.

"There's no one. Everyone is away or working."

"Then Thor will have to go with you," Grandmother said.

Thor didn't want to go with his grandfather. Saturday was his favorite day. At home, if his mother didn't chase him outside, he watched cartoons all day. Sometimes, he didn't even get out of his pajamas.

"I'm too little," he said.

"He's too little," Grandfather agreed. "He can't lift boxes or pull nets."

"He can help set nets," his grandmother said. "I helped my father when I was his age."

"It's too cold," Thor said.

"It's much too cold out," his grandfather agreed.

Thor looked out the window. There were icicles as long as his arm.

"It'll be warmer in the morning," Grandmother said. "He'll just have to wear long underwear, two pairs of socks, two pairs of pants, two shirts, a sweater, a jacket, gloves, and mittens and wrap a wool scarf around his face."

Grandmother went to Thor's closet and took out all the clothes he would need and stacked them in a pile.

"I'll miss my cartoons tomorrow," Thor cried. "Batman is going to rescue Gotham City from the Joker."

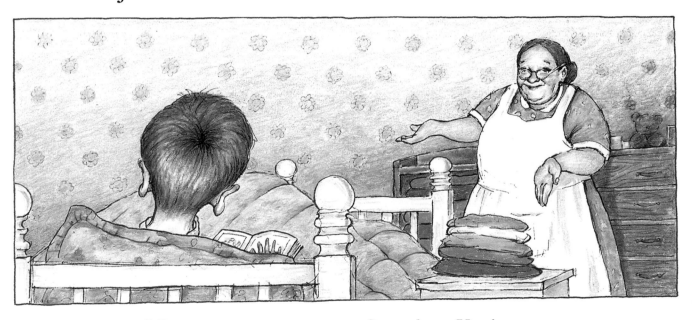

"Cartoons are on every Saturday. You've seen most of them once already anyway," Grandmother said. "Now, you'd better go to bed. We have to be up at six o'clock."

"I'll never see those cartoons again," Thor said as he was getting ready for bed.

It was still dark when Grandfather shook him awake. Thor rubbed the sleep from his eyes and began to put on all his clothes, but his grandfather told him not to put on the second pants, shirt, socks, and sweater until they were ready to leave. Otherwise, he'd be too warm.

Grandmother was already making breakfast. On the counter there were two lunch buckets and two thermoses. Grandfather and Thor ate their breakfast, then finished dressing and went outside. The snow was up to the top of the fences and as high as the windows. The snow was so cold it crunched under their feet like dried bread under Grandmother's rolling pin. Their breath made white clouds.

"Put your scarf over your mouth," Grandfather said. He handed Thor a strange-looking hat. "Your cap won't keep you warm. Put this on."

Thor looked at the hat. It was really a helmet. Like an aviator's helmet he'd seen on TV. It was leather with fur inside, and it had earflaps tied up on top. He put it on. His ears were cold so he untied the flaps and pulled them down and his grandfather tied them under his chin.

"That was mine when I was a boy," Grandfather said.

Thor's grandfather hooked up the caboose to the Bombardier. Then they loaded the caboose. As they worked Thor saw that there were still stars in the sky. When everything—the empty boxes, the boxes of nets, the stones they would use for anchors, the ropes, wood for the tin stove, ice chisels—was packed, Thor climbed into the Bombardier and knelt on the seat to look out.

The streets were deserted. Under the dark sky the high piles of snow were blue. Most of the houses were dark, but a few other fishermen were preparing to leave, and their lighted houses looked warm and inviting.

When Thor and Grandfather came to the beach, they stopped beside another Bombardier.

"Where's Ben?" one of the fishermen asked.

Grandfather explained that Ben was sick.

"No use taking that boy," the man said. "He'll blow away and you'll never find him."

"That's what I told his grandmother," Grandfather said. "But she said he'll do fine."

They drove onto the lake. Ahead of them was a long ice ridge as high as a house. It ran in the same direction as the shore.

"That's a pressure ridge," Grandfather said. "The ice expands and gets too big for the lake and pushes up. Just like the time you put your soft drink in the freezer and forgot it and it froze. It broke the bottle."

They couldn't go over or through the ice ridge. Instead, they drove beside it until they finally came to its end. When they went around it, the lake was flat and white as far as Thor could see.

"What if we fall through the ice?" he asked. He thought of his nice warm bed and how he should be waking up in an hour to watch television.

"There are dangerous places," his grandfather said. "That's where the current eats the ice from underneath and makes it thin. But we aren't going there. Where we fish, the ice is so strong it will hold a big truck."

The Bombardier was very noisy and bumped and banged, because in places the ice was rough. Behind them the shore disappeared, and Thor couldn't see land anywhere. There was just ice and more ice.

"How will we get back?" he said. He was remembering what the fisherman had said about his being blown away by the wind.

"The sun rises in the east. It sets in the west," Grandfather said. "The west side is where we live. We just go that way. Besides, we are leaving tracks behind. And we have a compass."

His grandfather stopped at a place where the ice was clear and dark, and Thor was afraid that it wouldn't be strong enough to hold them up. But then he remembered that his grandfather and Ben went out fishing every day and they never fell into the water.

The wind was blowing and snow was drifting around his ankles. The ice was slippery, and Thor wondered if he might actually blow away.

Just then there was a large booming noise like a huge explosion.

"What's that?" Thor asked.

"That's the ice cracking," Grandfather said. "Sometimes the ice pulls apart and leaves open water. We have to watch for cracks. We don't want to fall into them."

Grandfather started the auger at the side of the Bombardier. As it drilled through the ice, it made a lot of noise and ice chips flew everywhere. The auger made a clean round hole right to the water. Grandfather shoveled snow from around the hole.

"We have to set a gang of nets," Grandfather said, pointing at some boxes of nets. "We have to take them under the ice for eighty yards."

Thor tried to imagine how they could get nets under the ice. You couldn't push them because the nets weren't stiff. You couldn't pull them because the ice was in the way. He hoped his grandfather didn't expect him to get into the hole and swim under the ice with them. Aquaman could do that, but he couldn't.

"You see this?" Grandfather said. He held up a board with a spring and a piece of metal in the middle. "This is a jigger. It walks under the ice."

Grandfather pushed the jigger down the hole and under the ice. He had a running line attached. He pulled the running line, then let it go.

"When I pull, this piece of metal catches on the ice. When I let go it pushes the board forward. It'll pull the running line along. Your job is to walk above the jigger and listen. The ice is too thick to see it, but you can hear it. You have to listen closely. When the running line has gone eighty yards the jigger will stop. Then we'll dig a hole there."

Thor stood over where Grandfather had put the jigger. Grandfather pulled the running line and let go. Thor heard a click. Then another one.

Thor walked along the ice, listening carefully, leaning against the wind to keep from being blown away. He wondered if maybe he shouldn't have put some rocks in his pockets to keep his feet on the ice.

When the jigger stopped clicking, they dug a hole with the auger, but there was no jigger. Thor thought he'd made a mistake, but his grandfather just took a big metal hook and swept it under the ice in a circle. When he pulled it, the jigger popped into the hole.

They had the first gang of nets in the water and
were putting the empty net boxes into the caboose
when they heard a roar. Thor looked up. Four snow-
mobiles were racing over the lake.

Grandfather shook his head. "They shouldn't be doing that," he said. "They travel too fast and don't look where they're going. They can get into lots of trouble."

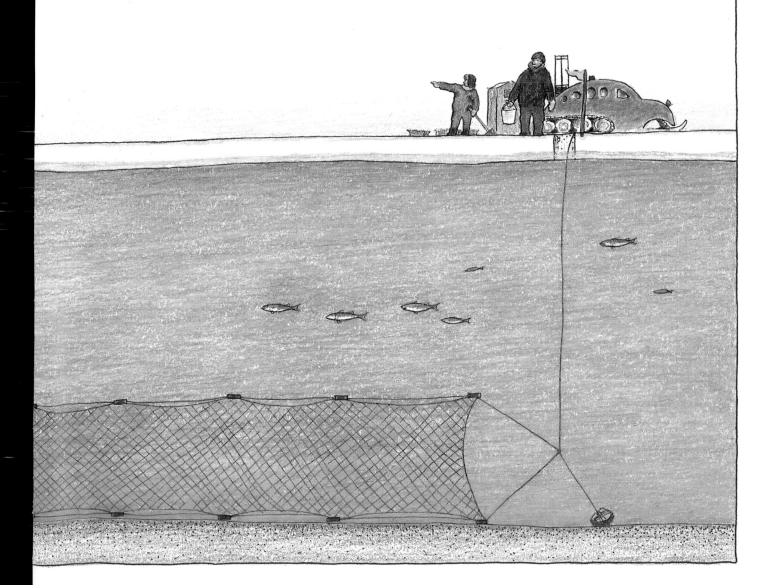

When they finished they sat inside the caboose and had their lunch.

As they started for shore Thor watched for cracks. In the distance he saw a flashing light. He pointed it out to his grandfather.

When they got close they saw that a large crack had opened up and the snowmobilers were on the far side. When they looked closer, they saw that a man had fallen into the water. He was on their side of the crack. As they watched he tried to pull himself up, but the ice broke and he disappeared.

"We've got to get him out," Grandfather said. "Get out on the ice. If you hear ice cracking, run away from the Bombardier."

Grandfather took a coil of rope and started toward the man in the water. About halfway there, there was a loud cracking and Thor ran away from the Bombardier, but it wasn't the ice under him that was breaking. It was the ice under his grandfather. His grandfather had to run back.

"The ice is too thin, Thor," Grandfather said. "And I'm too big and heavy. You're small and light. You're going to have to take the rope."

"Me?" Thor said. He was afraid. He could see the man's head in the water. A superhero could take the rope, but he wasn't a superhero.

"You do as I tell you and you'll be fine. I won't let anything happen to you," Grandfather said.

He tied a rope around Thor's waist. He gave Thor a second rope to take to the man. He made a noose in the end so the man could grab hold.

There were lots of small white cracks where his grandfather had walked. They gave a squeaking noise that made Thor shiver. When Thor got close to the man in the water, his grandfather yelled for him to lie down flat and to squirm forward. Thor lay down and pulled himself forward on his elbows, and when he got close, he threw the rope so it landed beside the man's hand. The man tried to pick it up but couldn't. His hands were so cold he couldn't close his fingers.

Thor looked at the black water and felt the ice move. He wanted to go back. There was ice on the man's face and hair. Thor wanted to get back in the Bombardier and race back to town and climb into bed.

"Help," the man said and lifted up one arm. He looked afraid.

Thor wiggled closer, then closer. He took the noose and pushed it over the man's arm and pulled it tight, then he squirmed backward.

Grandfather pulled the man up onto the ice, then along the ice to the caboose. They took off his clothes and dried him with a blanket, then put him into a sleeping bag Grandfather kept for emergencies and fed him hot cocoa from their thermoses.

After they took the man to the hospital, they drove home, clanking down the road.

"You're very late," Grandmother said. "I was worried something had gone wrong."

"Thor had a great adventure," Grandfather said. "He helped save someone's life."

"You're always teasing," Grandmother said.

Thor described all that had happened. As Grandmother listened she put out plates of rullapilsa and brown bread, smoked goldeye, and, for dessert, slices of vinetarta and ponnukokur. The ponnukokur were thin pancakes dusted with brown sugar and rolled up. They were Thor's favorite.

Some of the neighbors dropped by and the story had to be told all over again. Thor was so busy telling about his great adventure that he never mentioned his television programs once.

His grandfather said, "Thor's not big and he's not heavy and the wind might blow him away, but he can find the jigger and he's brave. I'd take him fishing with me anytime."

PONNUKOKUR

Ask a grown-up to help you make this Icelandic-Canadian treat of
Thor's.

2 eggs	1 mL (¼ tsp) baking soda
50 mL (¼ cup) sour cream	pinch salt
2 mL (½ tsp) vanilla	250 mL (1 cup) milk
175 mL (¾ cup) flour	25 mL (2 tbsp) butter
2 mL (½ tsp) baking powder	Brown sugar

1. In large bowl, whisk together eggs, sour cream, and vanilla.
2. Sift flour, baking powder, baking soda, and salt into small bowl.
3. Add sifted ingredients to egg mixture and whisk together well.
4. Gradually whisk in milk.
5. In small frying pan, melt butter. Add to batter and mix in well.
6. Pour just enough batter into frying pan to cover bottom. Cook,
lifting outer edge of pancake away from pan so that it doesn't burn.
When pancake is light brown on bottom, flip over and lightly cook
on second side. Set on plate to cool.
7. Continue cooking pancakes until all batter is used (you may
need to add a little more butter or oil to the pan to prevent
sticking).
Sprinkle each ponnukokur with brown sugar and roll into a tube.
These are to be eaten with your fingers.

Makes about 1 dozen ponnukokur